leapfrog

Cara's Breakfast

First published in 2007 by
Franklin Watts
338 Euston Road
London
NW1 3BH

Franklin Watts Australia
Level 17/207 Kent Street
Sydney
NSW 2000

A CIP catalogue record for this book is available
from the British Library.

ISBN 978 0 7496 7093 1 (hbk)
ISBN 978 0 7496 7797 8 (pbk)

Series Editor: Jackie Hamley
Series Advisor: Dr Barrie Wade
Series Designer: Peter Scoulding

Printed in China

Franklin Watts is a division of
Hachette Children's Books,
an Hachette Livre UK company.

Cara's Breakfast

by Jill Atkins

Illustrated by Gwyneth Williamson

W
FRANKLIN WATTS
LONDON•SYDNEY

Cara lived on a farm.

One morning, Cara asked
Dad, "Please can I have
an egg for breakfast?"

"Ask Hattie the hen," said Dad.

Cara ran to the
hen house.

"Please will you lay me an egg?" she asked Hattie.

"I'm hungry," Hattie clucked. "Fetch me some corn. Then I will."

So Cara ran to the barn.

"Please will you give me some corn?" she asked Mum.

"Fetch me some milk.
Then I will," said Mum.

So Cara ran to the milking shed.

"Please will you give me some milk?" she asked Daisy the cow.

"Fetch me some fresh grass. Then I will," mooed Daisy.

So Cara ran to the field and picked lots of fresh grass.

21

She hurried back to Daisy.
"Thanks!" Daisy mooed.

Then Daisy gave Cara
some milk.

Cara carried the milk
back to the barn.

"Thanks!" said Mum. Then she gave Cara some corn.

Corn

Cara ran back to the hen house. "Thanks!" clucked Hattie.

Cara waited and waited.
At last, Hattie laid an egg.
"Thanks!" said Cara.

Cara carried the egg inside. "Here's my egg for breakfast," she said.

"But it's lunch time now!"
laughed Dad.

Leapfrog has been specially designed to fit the requirements of the National Literacy Strategy. It offers real books for beginning readers by top authors and illustrators. There are 67 Leapfrog stories to choose from:

The Bossy Cockerel
ISBN 978 0 7496 3828 3

Bill's Baggy Trousers
ISBN 978 0 7496 3829 0

Little Joe's Big Race
ISBN 978 0 7496 3832 0

The Little Star
ISBN 978 0 7496 3833 7

The Cheeky Monkey
ISBN 978 0 7496 3830 6

Selfish Sophie
ISBN 978 0 7496 4385 0

Recycled!
ISBN 978 0 7496 4388 1

Felix on the Move
ISBN 978 0 7496 4387 4

Pippa and Poppa
ISBN 978 0 7496 4386 7

Jack's Party
ISBN 978 0 7496 4389 8

The Best Snowman
ISBN 978 0 7496 4390 4

Mary and the Fairy
ISBN 978 0 7496 4633 2

The Crying Princess
ISBN 978 0 7496 4632 5

Jasper and Jess
ISBN 978 0 7496 4081 1

The Lazy Scarecrow
ISBN 978 0 7496 4082 8

The Naughty Puppy
ISBN 978 0 7496 4383 6

Big Bad Blob
ISBN 978 0 7496 7092 4*
ISBN 978 0 7496 7796 1

Cara's Breakfast
ISBN 978 0 7496 7093 1*
ISBN 978 0 7496 7797 8

Why Not?
ISBN 978 0 7496 7094 8*
ISBN 978 0 7496 7798 5

Croc's Tooth
ISBN 978 0 7496 7095 5*
ISBN 978 0 7496 7799 2

The Magic Word
ISBN 978 0 7496 7096 2*
ISBN 978 0 7496 7800 5

Tim's Tent
ISBN 978 0 7496 7097 9*
ISBN 978 0 7496 7801 2

FAIRY TALES
Cinderella
ISBN 978 0 7496 4228 0

The Three Little Pigs
ISBN 978 0 7496 4227 3

Jack and the Beanstalk
ISBN 978 0 7496 4229 7

The Three Billy Goats Gruff
ISBN 978 0 7496 4226 6

Goldilocks and the Three Bears
ISBN 978 0 7496 4225 9

Little Red Riding Hood
ISBN 978 0 7496 4224 2

Rapunzel
ISBN 978 0 7496 6159 5

Snow White
ISBN 978 0 7496 6161 8

The Emperor's New Clothes
ISBN 978 0 7496 6163 2

The Pied Piper of Hamelin
ISBN 978 0 7496 6164 9

Hansel and Gretel
ISBN 978 0 7496 6162 5

The Sleeping Beauty
ISBN 978 0 7496 6160 1

Rumpelstiltskin
ISBN 978 0 7496 6165 6

The Ugly Duckling
ISBN 978 0 7496 6166 3

Puss in Boots
ISBN 978 0 7496 6167 0

The Frog Prince
ISBN 978 0 7496 6168 7

The Princess and the Pea
ISBN 978 0 7496 6169 4

Dick Whittington
ISBN 978 0 7496 6170 0

The Elves and the Shoemaker
ISBN 978 0 7496 6581 4

The Little Match Girl
ISBN 978 0 7496 6582 1

The Little Mermaid
ISBN 978 0 7496 6583 8

The Little Red Hen
ISBN 978 0 7496 6585 2

The Nightingale
ISBN 978 0 7496 6586 9

Thumbelina
ISBN 978 0 7496 6587 6

RHYME TIME
Mr Spotty's Potty
ISBN 978 0 7496 3831 3

Eight Enormous Elephants
ISBN 978 0 7496 4634 9

Freddie's Fears
ISBN 978 0 7496 4382 9

Squeaky Clean
ISBN 978 0 7496 6805 1

Craig's Crocodile
ISBN 978 0 7496 6806 8

Felicity Floss: Tooth Fairy
ISBN 978 0 7496 6807 5

Captain Cool
ISBN 978 0 7496 6808 2

Monster Cake
ISBN 978 0 7496 6809 9

The Super Trolley Ride
ISBN 978 0 7496 6810 5

The Royal Jumble Sale
ISBN 978 0 7496 6811 2

But, Mum!
ISBN 978 0 7496 6812 9

Dan's Gran's Goat
ISBN 978 0 7496 6814 3

Lighthouse Mouse
ISBN 978 0 7496 6815 0

Big Bad Bart
ISBN 978 0 7496 6816 7

Ron's Race
ISBN 978 0 7496 6817 4

Woolly the Bully
ISBN 978 0 7496 7098 6*
ISBN 978 0 7496 7790 9

Boris the Spider
ISBN 978 0 7496 7099 3*
ISBN 978 0 7496 7791 6

Miss Polly's Seaside Brolly
ISBN 978 0 7496 7100 6*
ISBN 978 0 7496 7792 3

The Lonely Pirate
ISBN 978 0 7496 7101 3*
ISBN 978 0 7496 7793 0

What a Frog!
ISBN 978 0 7496 7102 0*
ISBN 978 0 7496 7794 7

Juggling Joe
ISBN 978 0 7496 7103 7*
ISBN 978 0 7496 7795 4

* hardback

This book belongs to:

Olivia Perrin

Retold by Monica Hughes
Illustrated by Adrienne Salgado

Reading consultants: Betty Root and Monica Hughes

Marks and Spencer p.l.c.
PO Box 3339
Chester, CH99 9QS

shop online
www.marksandspencer.com

ISBN 978-1-84461-814-9
Printed in China

First
Readers

Read Together

Rapunzel

**MARKS &
SPENCER**

Helping your child to read

First Readers are closely linked to the National Curriculum. Their vocabulary has been carefully selected from the word lists recommended by the National Literacy Strategy.

Read the story

Read the story
to your child
a few times.

Soon Rapunzel grew into a beautiful
girl with long, long hair.
The witch took Rapunzel to a tower
The tower had one window.
But there was no door.
Rapunzel lived alone in the tower.
Every day she sat at the window
singing.

14

Follow your finger

Run your finger under
the text as you read.
Your child will soon begin to
follow the words with you.

Look at the pictures

Talk about the pictures. They will help your child to understand the story.

The witch took Rapunzel to a tower.

15

Have a go

Let your child have a go at reading the large type on each right-hand page. It repeats a line from the story.

Join in

When your child is ready, encourage them to join in with the main story text. Shared reading is the first step to reading alone.

Once there was a man and his wife.
The wife was going to have a baby.
But sadly she was ill.
A witch lived next door.
The witch had a garden.
It was full of rapunzel plants.
The leaves were good to eat.

The witch had a garden.

9

"I must eat rapunzel leaves or I will
die," said the wife.
So the man went into the witch's
garden.
The man picked the leaves.
His wife ate the leaves and she did
not die.
The man picked the leaves every day.

The man picked the leaves.

One day the witch saw him.
"Why are you stealing my leaves?"
she said.
"My wife must eat them or she will die,"
said the man.
"You can have my leaves," said the witch,
"but you must give me your baby."

Soon the baby was born.
The baby was called Rapunzel.
The man gave the baby to the witch.

He gave the baby to the witch.

Soon Rapunzel grew into a beautiful
girl with long, long hair.
The witch took Rapunzel to a tower.
The tower had one window.
But there was no door.
Rapunzel lived alone in the tower.
Every day she sat at the window
singing.

The witch took Rapunzel
to a tower.

Every day the witch came to the tower
and called,

"Rapunzel, Rapunzel,
Let down your hair."

Rapunzel let down her long hair.
Then the witch climbed up
Rapunzel's hair.

"Rapunzel, Rapunzel,
Let down your hair."

One day a prince came by.
He heard Rapunzel singing.
He wanted to get into the tower.
But there was no door.

Then the prince saw the witch.
He heard her say,

> "Rapunzel, Rapunzel,
> Let down your hair."

He saw her climb up Rapunzel's hair.

When the witch went away, the
prince said,

> "Rapunzel, Rapunzel,
> Let down your hair."

The prince climbed up Rapunzel's hair.

The prince climbed up.

Every time the witch went away the
prince came to see Rapunzel.

One day Rapunzel told the witch about
the prince.
The witch was very angry.
"I will cut off your hair," said the witch.
The witch cut off Rapunzel's hair.
Then the witch sent Rapunzel away.

"I will cut off your hair," said
the witch.

The prince came to the tower.
He did not hear Rapunzel singing.
But he said,

"Rapunzel, Rapunzel,
Let down your hair."

The witch let down Rapunzel's hair.
The prince climbed up Rapunzel's hair.

The witch let down
Rapunzel's hair.

When the prince got to the window he
saw the witch.
The witch was very angry.
She let go of Rapunzel's hair.
The prince fell down.
He fell into a thorn bush.
The thorns went in his eyes and he
could not see.

The prince fell down.

The prince walked for days.
Then he heard someone singing.
It was Rapunzel!
The prince told her about the witch.
Rapunzel cried.
Her tears fell into the prince's eyes.
They washed away the thorns.
The prince could see!

The prince and Rapunzel were married
and they all lived happily ever after.

The prince and Rapunzel were
married.

Look back in your book.

Can you read these words?

Rapunzel

witch

tower

prince

baby

Can you answer these questions?

Who gave the baby
to the witch?

Where did Rapunzel live?

Who cut off
Rapunzel's hair?

First Readers

(subject to availability)

Beauty and the Beast
Cinderella
The Elves and the Shoemaker
The Emperor's New Clothes
The Enormous Turnip
The Gingerbread Man
Goldilocks and the Three Bears
Hansel and Gretel
Jack and the Beanstalk
Little Red Riding Hood
The Princess and the Pea
Rapunzel
Rumpelstiltskin
Sleeping Beauty
Snow White and the Seven Dwarfs
The Three Billy Goats Gruff
The Three Little Pigs
The Ugly Duckling